the thanking you sharks

by giles andreae

original illustrations by janet cronin

EGMONT

EGMONT

We bring stories to life

First published in Great Britain 2011 by Egmont UK Limited
239 Kensington High Street, London W8 6SA

Text copyright © Portobello Rights Limited 2011
Illustrations © Portobello Rights Limited and the BBC 2011,
taken from the BBC series 'World of Happy by Giles Andreae'
based on original illustrations by Janet Cronin

Giles Andreae has asserted his moral rights

A CIP catalogue record for this title is available from the British Library

ISBN 978 1 4052 5847 0
1 3 5 7 9 10 8 6 4 2
Printed in Italy

a story about GOOD MANNERS

my name is ....

and polite words I am good at using are

....

....

....

The GREEDY sharks swam swiftly through the water . . .

consuming every
little fish that came
their way.

BELCH!

And after each sweet morsel, these sharks would BELCH as loudly as could be.

But then one shark declared, "I don't mean to cause TROUBLE but what if, after every meal, we all said THANKING YOU instead?"

"We cannot CHANGE our diet,
for sharks are sharks and
fish are what we eat ..."

"But all these little fishes are giving up their LIVES for us, and surely that deserves our full RESPECT?"

nod

The greedy sharks fell quiet, until another said, "He's RIGHT. My friend, I'm with you," and he ate a fish.

"Gulp! Thanking you," he said.

thanking you!

"How WONDERFUL you sound," the first shark offered. "How noble, and how . . . GENEROUS inside."

"That little fish was HAPPY to be eaten. All creatures need their DIGNITY and PRIDE."

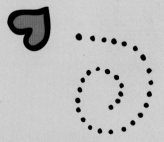

And now ALL sharks
say THANKING YOU
when they have eaten.

thanking you!

But they TRY.